Cutiecorns

Join the Cutiecorns on every adventure!

Heart of Gold

Purrfect Pranksters

Rainy Day Rescue

Carnival Chaos

Carnival Chaos

by Shannon Penney
illustrated by Addy Rivera Sonda

SCHOLASTIC INC.

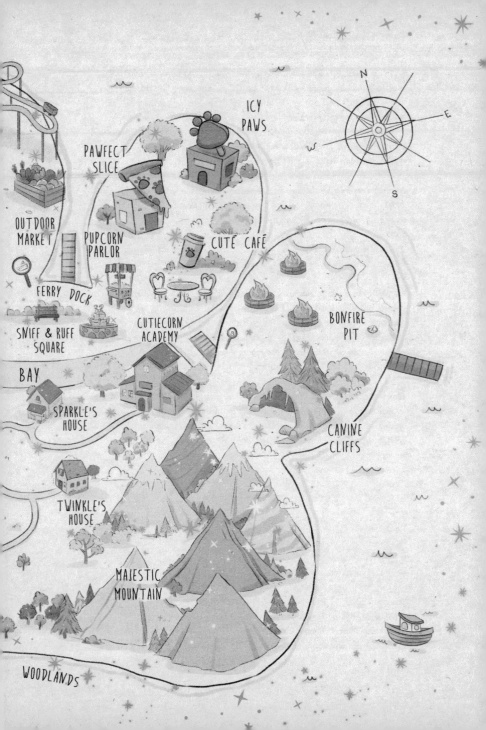

This book is a work of fiction. Names, characters, places, and incidents are either the product of the author's imagination or are used fictitiously, and any resemblance to actual persons, living or dead, business establishments, events, or locales is entirely coincidental.

ISBN 978-1-338-54048-2
10 9 8 7 6 5 4 3 2 1   21 22 23 24 25

Printed in the U.S.A. 40
First printing 2021

Book design by Jennifer Rinaldi

Scholastic Inc., 557 Broadway, New York, NY 10012
Scholastic UK Ltd., Euston House,
24 Eversholt Street, London NW1 1DB
Made in Jefferson City, U.S.A.

Chapter 1

"Bow wow, Sparkle, that was puptastic!" Twinkle cheered, clapping her paws. On either side of her, her friends Glitter and Flash barked and whooped in agreement.

Up onstage, Sparkle took a graceful bow. Her golden fur shimmered in the spotlight— and so did the golden horn between her ears. After all, Sparkle, Twinkle, and their friends weren't regular puppies. They were Cutiecorns! The colorful horns on their heads gave them pawsome magical powers. But Sparkle had just wowed them with no magic at all!

"I had no idea you could sing like that!" Glitter said, giving Sparkle a hug as she stepped down from the stage.

"Me neither," Flash barked, racing in excited circles. "That was incrediwoof!"

Sparkle blushed, but a happy smile stretched across her snout. "Thanks! I've been practicing doggone hard."

"This talent show is going to be the best thing Puppypaw Island has ever seen!" Flash cried. "Just think how impressed our visitors will be!"

Twinkle couldn't help grinning at her friend's enthusiasm. Flash never missed an opportunity to yap on and on about something! Even though Twinkle pretended to be grumpy about it sometimes, it was one of the things she liked best about the little Yorkshire

Terrier—she was a bundle of energy and excitement! Plus, the talent show was definitely something to bark about.

"It *is* pretty ter-ruff-ic that we get to host Cutiecorns from far and wide this weekend," Twinkle said with a nod.

Sparkle danced on her paws. "Yup, turns out something good did come from those mischievous little kittens who showed up here! Everyone wants to get to know one another a little better," she said. "The first-ever Cutiecorn Carnival and Talent Show is going to be a grrrrreat success. I just know it!"

Twinkle peered around the auditorium from her seat in the first row. In front of her was an impressive stage with heavy red curtains and bright lights. Behind her, rows of padded seats stretched on and on into the darkness. Of all the rooms at the pups' school, Cutiecorn Academy, Twinkle thought this one must be the grandest. It was nice of Mrs. Horne, the head of the school, to let them stay after and practice on the big stage!

"My turn," Glitter said quietly, climbing up the steps. She cued some music, took a deep breath, and began dancing, twirling, and leaping across the stage. Twinkle knew that her friend had been taking ballet lessons ever since she was a little pup, but she'd had no idea that Glitter had turned into such a barking good ballerina!

Sparkle and Flash both looked at Twinkle with wide eyes. They were surprised, too!

When the music faded, Glitter posed

pawfectly still for a moment. Then she curt-
sied as her friends erupted into a flurry of
barks and cheers.

"You're so graceful!"

"Hot dog, what a performance!"

"You're a puptastic ballerina!"

This time, it was Glitter's turn to blush as
she stepped down from the stage. "I love to

dance," she said with a happy sigh. "It's my favorite thing in the whole world!"

Twinkle smiled along with the rest of her friends, but inside, she felt her heart squeeze a little. It would be nice to have something she enjoyed doing that much! Twinkle didn't really have any special talents. She worked hard at learning her magic and being a good friend, and there were plenty of things she liked to do—there just wasn't anything that made her stand out.

She felt Glitter's paw on her shoulder. "Are you sure you don't want to perform in the talent show, Twinkle?" the little white Maltese asked quietly. Glitter was especially good at caring magic. She could tune in to Twinkle's feelings better than anyone! Twinkle should have known that her smile wouldn't fool Glitter.

"Oh, I'm sure," Twinkle said with a shrug. "I don't like the spotlight. The idea of getting up in front of so many Cutiecorns is totally fur-raising!"

Sparkle shuddered. "I hear what you're barking," she said. "Just thinking about performing in front of a big crowd tomorrow makes my stomach do flip-flops!"

"Don't worry," Twinkle reassured her friend. "I'll be right here in the front row, cheering you on. Just look for this friendly snout!" She flashed a huge, silly smile, and the rest of the pups all dissolved into giggles.

Flash jumped to her paws and raced onto the stage. "Ladies and gentlepups," she announced in a booming voice, "now presenting the one, the only, Flash the Magnificent!" She winked. "Lucky for you, she's not nervous at all."

With that, Flash launched into a woof-tastic gymnastics and acrobatic display, full of flips, tumbles, and even paws-free juggling! (Flash was best at shifting magic, and she'd been working hard to use only her magic to move the balls through the air. Twinkle had to admit, it was a spectacular sight!)

Down in the audience, Twinkle, Glitter, and Sparkle clapped and howled. Twinkle couldn't help giggling. Even though she still felt a little left out of the talent show, she was lucky to have friends who always made her feel wanted, no matter what. And they had the whole Cutiecorn Carnival to look forward to, not just the talent show.

Bow wow, it was going to be an exciting few days!

Chapter 2

Once Flash had finished practicing her performance, the four friends headed for the Furmusement Park. There was so much to do to prepare for the big weekend, and the pups were ready to lend a paw!

As they trotted through Barking Bay and toward the water's edge, Twinkle couldn't help marveling at how many pups were out and about. It seemed like all of Puppypaw Island was helping prepare! Pups were cleaning, hanging decorations, and arranging big pots of colorful flowers. Some of the adult Cutiecorns used their magic to get the job done, while others worked by paw. Twinkle still felt a rush of excitement every time she saw magic at work, even if it was just a mop moving across the cobblestones on its own!

Twinkle's mom had been helping to organize the whole weekend, so Twinkle knew just how much work went into it. Since their guests would be arriving first thing in the morning, now it was all paws on deck!

"Hey, pups!" A Collie with a bright green horn waved from the side of the main

walkway. He held a roll of bright blue streamers in his other paw.

"Hi, Fuzz!" Sparkle barked, trotting over
to their classmate with her friends on her tail.
"Need some help?"

Fuzz grinned. "Fur sure! We're just hanging streamers between these lampposts, all
along the walkway to the Furmusement Park."
He pointed a paw a bit farther along. "Flip
and Scooter are down that way. Maybe you
guys can start on the other side of the
walkway?"

"You bet!" Flash yipped, bouncing on her
paws. She grabbed an armful of streamers and
tossed a colorful roll to each of her friends.
"Dibs on purple, to match my horn!"

Twinkle rolled her eyes, giggling. She climbed up on a railing, pausing to tilt her face toward the blue sky. The sun felt so good on her fur! Twinkle and her friends had gotten caught in a massive storm not long ago, so she was especially grateful that the weather was so beautiful for carnival weekend.

Flash danced back and forth along a

railing, using her shifting magic to twist and twirl her streamers overhead. "There are a lot of exciting things about this weekend, but the best part is going to be meeting all the different Cutiecorns, paws down!"

Glitter smiled, tying the end of her streamer around a lamppost. "Other than those rascally kittens who stowed away on your dad's boat,

Flash, I've never met any Cutiecorns that weren't pups before." Flash's dad was an explorer. He often traveled to far-off places and met all different kinds of Cutiecorns. The last time he'd gone on an adventure, four Cutiecorn kittens had come back with him—and caused chaos all over Puppypaw Island with their magic!

"Me neither," Sparkle said thoughtfully. "Twinkle, has your mom told you who is officially coming?"

Twinkle nodded. They'd sent out lots of invitations to Cutiecorns far and wide! "Just about everyone we invited is planning to come—bunnies, hedgehogs, birds, hamsters, cats, and goats. The sea Cutiecorns, like the dolphins, can't really be on land long enough to attend the carnival, but it sounds like they were happy to be invited anyway." Twinkle felt a little flutter of excitement in her belly just talking about it . . . and some nerves, too!

Flash did a backflip off the railing, landing on her paws with a flourish. "Goats? I've heard they'll eat *anything*! My dad once had a pair of binoculars that turned into a goat's lunch!"

The other pups laughed. Twinkle giggled along with them, but she couldn't shake that feeling in her belly. All of these different Cutiecorns probably had different customs, traditions, and behaviors, too. Would they all be able to get along on Puppypaw Island together? Twinkle's mind spun with things that could go wrong: Goats eating all the ride tickets! Hedgehogs accidentally popping all the balloons! And what if the mischievous kittens came back?

A familiar bark interrupted Twinkle's thoughts. "Look at all these helpful paws over here!" Twinkle's mom walked up with a clipboard and a big grin. "Now I can mark down that the streamers are almost all hung up and ready to go, thanks to you."

"How's the rest of the setup going?" Glitter asked.

"Furbulously!" Twinkle's mom said. "The Furmusement Park is all set up for a full day of fun tomorrow. There will be more food, rides, and games than you can shake your snout at. I'm heading over to the auditorium now, to make sure we're ready for tomorrow night's talent show. With all the different Cutiecorns we have joining us, it's going to be a full house!"

Sparkle's eyes widened at the mention of a big, packed auditorium. She swallowed hard. Glitter put a paw around her shoulders, and Twinkle gave her an encouraging smile. Flash, meanwhile, couldn't keep her paws still. She raced circles around Twinkle's mom, barking excitedly about their performances.

Twinkle's mom laughed. "Hot dog, I can't wait to see!" She waved a paw as she trotted off down the walkway. "Keep it up, pups—see you for dinner, Twinkle!"

Twinkle and her friends waved back.

"I think I'm too excited to eat dinner tonight," Glitter said, wagging her tail.

"Plus, you have to save room," Flash barked. "Just think of all the carnival food we'll have tomorrow! Cotton candy and ice cream and french fries and fried dough . . ."

Twinkle clutched her belly, laughing. "Bow wow, you're giving me a stomachache!"

Chapter 3

The next morning, Twinkle woke with a start. Her eyes popped open, and then she squinted at the bright sunshine streaming through her window. Hot dog, it was carnival day!

Twinkle leaped to her paws. Cutiecorns from far and wide were due to start arriving soon, and she wanted to be there to greet them!

She raced down to the empty kitchen,

grabbing a granola bar from the counter. Her most prized possession, the golden charm bracelet she'd gotten at the Enchanted Jubilee, jingled on her wrist. She glanced down at it, admiring the charms that dangled there. Each one reminded her of a different adventure where she'd learned to use her magic!

Happy barks and laughs echoed outside in the yard. Twinkle stepped out the back door and spotted her dad pushing her younger twin siblings, Tumble and Trot, on the tire swing that hung from the big old maple tree.

"Good morning!" her dad called, waving a paw. "These two rascals have been up for hours, so we moved the party outside." He rolled his eyes dramatically, and Twinkle

giggled. She definitely got her eye-rolling skills from her dad.

"Higher, Daddy! Higher!" Tumble cried, her ears flapping in the breeze.

Twinkle glanced around the yard. "Did Mom already leave?"

"You bet your bark she did," her dad said.

"She and her clipboard were out of here at the crack of dawn. It's a big day!"

Twinkle nodded, bouncing on her paws with a combination of excitement and nerves. It *was* a big day! Who knew what might happen? Like her mom, Twinkle enjoyed being prepared for what was coming. But how could she possibly prepare for meeting so many new and different Cutiecorns?

"I think I'll head down to the docks," she said. "I want to be there when the boats start arriving."

Her dad grinned. "Can't wait to meet our guests, huh?" He ruffled her fur. "Go on, then. I'm sure you'll find Mom down there. We'll join you at the carnival a little later!" He lowered his voice to a whisper. "If we go too early, these crazy pups will eat all the cotton candy before the carnival even gets started."

"Cotton candy?" Trot yipped. "Did you say cotton candy?"

"Get out while you still can!" Twinkle's dad whispered with a wink.

Laughing and blowing kisses to her brother and sister, Twinkle raced around to the front of the house and down the lane. She ran as fast as her paws would take her, kicking up a cloud of dust in her wake. It felt good to run! When her paws were pounding against the dirt, Twinkle could ignore the funny fluttering feeling in her belly.

"Hey, wait up!" a familiar voice barked behind her. Flash darted up, with Glitter right on her tail. Flash coughed dramatically, waving a paw in front of her snout. "Bow wow, Twinkle, it was like a dirt tornado behind you!"

Twinkle laughed and helped brush the dirt from Flash's fur. "Sorry! I'm just excited to get down to the docks."

"Carnival day is finally here!" Glitter said, giving Twinkle a sweet smile. Twinkle knew that, even without using her magic, her friend could tell she was nervous. But as always, having Glitter by her side made Twinkle feel better!

"Hey, pups! Are you coming, or what?" Sparkle's bark carried from farther down the lane. "I can hear you woofing away up there!"

The other pups giggled and raced off down the hill. "Catch us if you can!" Flash cried, breezing right by Sparkle. Sparkle jumped to her paws and took off, barking and laughing all the way.

Before long, the four friends reached the main docks. They plopped down, panting. "Next time we decide to do that, remind me that I don't really like to run," Twinkle said with a smirk.

Pausing to catch their breaths, the pups looked around. What a pawsome sight! The docks were bustling with pups of all ages, ready to greet their guests. Streamers lined the docks and the walkway as far as the eye could see. Colorful balloons bobbed from every lamppost, and the water glistened in the morning sunlight. The air rang with excited barks and chatter.

Twinkle caught sight of her mom, standing

at the end of the longest wooden dock. She waved a paw, and her mom waved back with a ter-ruff-ically big smile on her snout.

Suddenly, a low, long sound cut through the air. The pups all looked at one another with wide eyes.

"That sounds like a boat horn!" Sparkle

woofed, standing on her tiptoes to get a better view.

Sure enough, a big green ship was approaching Puppypaw Island from one direction, and a yellow ship from another. Far on the horizon, Twinkle could make out two or three others. She pointed a paw, nudging her friends. It was happening! Their guests were arriving!

The pups watched breathlessly. The green ship drew closer and closer, giving Twinkle and her friends a clearer view. It was like no ship Twinkle had ever seen! The decks were covered with thick grass, and flowering vines twisted around the railings.

"Look!" Flash cried. "See the name?"

The name of the ship was painted in swirling

white letters along the side: HOPALONG EXPRESS.

A murmur ran through the crowd as all the pups peered intently at the ship. There were no passengers in sight! What kind of Cutiecorns would ride on a ship like that one?

Twinkle could feel her heart pounding. "Do you think it's—"

"Bunnies!" Glitter barked as fuzzy little faces, colorful horns, and tall, pointy ears appeared over the railing.

Chapter 4

Twinkle's heart thudded as the *Hopalong Express* pulled alongside the dock and coasted to a stop. Glitter and Sparkle stood close on either side of her, while Flash danced around them, jumping to try and get a better view of the bunnies.

Dozens of bunnies grinned and waved shyly from the boat. There were bigger adults and smaller kids, all with dazzling, colorful horns! Some of the bunnies had floppy ears, while others had ears that stood straight up. Twinkle had to smile at the way they twitched their noses.

"My mom said the different Cutiecorns will stay on their boats until everyone has docked," Twinkle told her friends. "Then

they'll all disembark for the Welcome Parade down to the Furmusement Park."

Glitter sighed happily. "It's so puptastically exciting!"

Over the next half hour, the pups watched as boat after boat docked in Barking Bay harbor. The hamsters' boat was the smallest, and was covered with clear tubes and spinning wheels for the tiny hamsters to run in. The hedgehogs were all snuggled up in nests on their boat, which was dark and shaded. Twinkle remembered her mom mentioning that hedgehogs were nocturnal, so they usually slept during the day! The goats arrived next, jumping and bounding around their multi-tiered boat. Many goats were perched on the highest tier, looking down at the crowds

below. Then came the cats, who walked effort-
lessly on the thin railings of their boat, looking
sleek and graceful.

"Is that everyone?" Sparkle wondered
aloud.

Glitter pointed a paw. "Almost—look!"

Off in the distance, the pups could see something high in the blue sky. It came closer by the
moment, and soon Twinkle realized just what
it was—a flock of colorful Cutiecorn birds!
Birds of every color and size flapped their wings
in perfect unison, swooping through the air.
They landed in a neat row along the top of the
WELCOME, CUTIECORNS! banner hanging
above the docks.

"Bow wow!" Flash cried. "That was totally
pawsome!"

Welcome, Cutiecorns!

Twinkle had to agree . . . but she was so overwhelmed and excited that she could hardly bark! These animals hadn't even set paw (or claw or hoof) on Puppypaw Island yet, and already it was clear that they were all completely different—from the pups, and from one another. Just the thought of it made Twinkle's snout spin a little.

A trumpet sounded, and Twinkle heard her mom's bark, amplified with her magic so that it sounded like she was using a megaphone. "To all our honored guests: Welcome to Puppypaw Island and the first annual Cutiecorn Carnival!" The crowd barked wildly, and the Cutiecorns on the boats all cheered. "We're ter-ruff-ically excited to have you join us. Now, if you're ready to disembark, you can head straight out that way for the Welcome Parade!"

The pups at the docks all began to step aside, lining the sides of the walkway and leaving the center clear for the parade. Twinkle, Sparkle, Flash, and Glitter got a spot right up front so they could see the Cutiecorn visitors clearly without having to peek around grown-ups' heads and horns.

First up were the birds, who darted and swooped overhead, wowing everyone along the parade route with their fancy flying. At times, they just looked like colorful blurs against the brilliant blue sky. The cats pranced proudly along the street, holding their heads and tails high. The hamsters ran behind them, their tiny legs moving extra-fast in order to keep up.

"They're so cute and fuzzy!" Glitter whispered to Twinkle. Next were the bunnies, hopping cheerfully and waving to the pups on the sidelines. Twinkle spotted a skittish little gray bunny near the back of the pack. She wasn't waving, and seemed to be ducking behind some of the bigger bunnies. As the others continued bouncing along, the little bunny fell farther and farther behind, until she was back among the goats, who clip-clopped along loudly.

Twinkle could see the look of panic on the little bunny's face, but no one else seemed to have noticed. Without another thought, Twinkle raced out onto the parade route.

"Hey, where are you going?" Twinkle could hear Flash bark behind her, but there was no time to reply.

Twinkle wound her way carefully through the goats until she reached the little bunny. "Hi," she said gently. "I'm Twinkle. Would you like some help getting back to your mom?"

Wide-eyed, the bunny nodded quickly.

"What's your name?" Twinkle asked.

The bunny whispered, "Fluff."

Twinkle crouched down. "Climb onto my back, Fluff, and I'll bring you to your mom in two shakes of a pup's tail." She winked and gave the bunny a reassuring smile. She knew that asking Fluff to climb onto her back was risky. After all, this little bunny had never seen a pup before, never mind ridden on one! But Twinkle also knew that the other animals in the parade were moving too quickly. Fluff would never be able to catch up on her own!

After a moment's hesitation, Fluff scrambled onto Twinkle's back. Twinkle could feel her trembling.

"Don't worry," she said. "I'll take it nice and slow, pup's honor!"

Twinkle walked out to the edge of the parade route and trotted along carefully, light on her paws. She passed the goats and caught up with the bunnies. She was about to ask Fluff which bunny was her mom, when she felt her horn begin to glow. Her seeing magic was kicking in! Suddenly, she noticed a larger gray bunny near the front of the pack. Twinkle knew, without a doubt, that it was the bunny she was looking for.

She approached slowly, not wanting to spook anyone. "I'll let you off right here," she whispered to Fluff. "You can head back to your mom, and she'll never know you were gone!"

Fluff slid down to the ground and gave

Twinkle a sheepish grin. "Thanks," she said, wiggling her tiny pink nose. She fell into line behind her mom, hopping happily and even waving a little paw to the pups on the sidelines.

Twinkle trotted back to her friends just in time to see the hedgehogs go rolling by. They had curled up into spiky little balls! All the pups clapped their paws and giggled.

"It was really nice of you to help that bunny," Glitter said quietly to Twinkle, patting her paw as they watched the parade move on down the street.

Twinkle blushed, but a smile stretched across her snout. "I could tell she was scared, being all alone in this strange new place. If

I'm feeling nervous about the carnival, just imagine how our visitors are feeling! It was like my magic told me what to do."

Glitter smiled sweetly. "I have a feeling your seeing magic is going to be working overtime today!"

Chapter 5

As the visiting Cutiecorns continued along the walkway to the Furmusement Park, the pups on the sidelines fell into step behind them. Everyone was barking with excitement!

"Did you see those spiky hedgehogs?" Flash cried, running circles around her friends. "I'm not sure I want to go near their quills, but maybe they'd let me use my shifting magic to move them around!"

Glitter's eyes grew wide, and she stopped in her tracks. "Flash, you can't just start moving our guests with your magic!"

Sparkle grinned and nudged her friend. "I think Flash was joking. Right?" She gave Flash a pointed look.

Flash shrugged. "I guess. But, you guys, I could use my magic to juggle the hedgehogs! Wouldn't that be puptastic?" The smile on her snout stretched from ear to ear.

"Flash!" Glitter barked indignantly.

"Don't forget," Twinkle said with a wink, "each of our guests has magic of their own. Who knows what they might do if you try to juggle them?"

Flash looked thoughtful. Then she cringed. "Pawsome point, Twinkle. I'll keep my magic to myself!"

Twinkle, Sparkle, and Glitter exchanged relieved looks as Flash bounded on ahead.

Before long, the pups spotted the bright lights of the Furmusement Park. Cheerful music played as they stepped under the archway and set paw into the park. Bow wow, what a sight!

"I've never seen the Furmusement Park so crowded before!" Sparkle barked.

Twinkle nodded in agreement. The carnival was already in full swing—and it was packed! The rides and game booths were all full of Cutiecorns, and the lines were long. Everywhere Twinkle looked, there was something new to see. Bunnies were chatting with hedgehogs. Goats and hamsters were telling jokes. Pups were giving kittens a paw up onto different rides. Birds were looping and swooping overhead.

How pawsitively exciting . . . and over-whelming!

"What should we do first?" Twinkle asked, turning to her friends.

Glitter woofed up. "I'd love a chance to chat with some of these other Cutiecorns."

"Now you're barking!" Flash said. "After all, Twinkle already got to meet a bunny. I want to meet a bunny! Or a hamster! Or a goat! Or—"

Twinkle laughed. "We get it, we get it!" She pointed a paw. "Let's get in line for the

carousel. It's right in the middle of the park,
so we'll be able to see everything while we
wait. And there are lots of other Cutiecorns in
line already!"

The four friends walked over to the carousel and stood at the back of the line. A pair of
little golden hamsters with blue horns turned
and glanced at them shyly.

"Hi," Glitter said sweetly. "I'm Glitter, and these are my friends Twinkle, Flash, and Sparkle. Welcome to Puppypaw Island! Are you having fun so far?"

The hamsters nodded, their little heads bobbing up and down quickly. When they squeaked up, their voices were high . . . and impawsibly fast! "Oh, yes! It's furbulous here! There's so much to see!" one remarked.

"We've never been away from Fur Hollow before, and our boat ride was such an adventure!" the other hamster squeaked.

"They talk so fast that it's kind of like talking to Flash," Twinkle muttered to Sparkle with a grin.

Just then, Flash jumped in. "We're so glad you're here!" she barked. "I'm Flash, and I have shifting magic. That means I can use my magic to move things. What does your magic do?"

The hamsters both sat up on their back legs, wiggling excitedly. "We use shifting magic, too!" one cried. "Watch this!" Within seconds, his horn began to glow, and he lifted the other hamster into the air overhead. She wiggled and giggled, waving down at them.

Flash's eyes lit up.

"Don't even think about it!" Twinkle whispered. "We're not juggling our guests, remember?"

Flash wrinkled her snout and sighed. "Oh, fine. It would be a barking good trick, though!"

As Flash, Glitter, and Sparkle continued chatting with the two little hamsters, Twinkle gazed around the busy carnival. There were so many smiling faces! Different Cutiecorns were having friendly conversations, while laughs and happy squeals rang out from the rides. But as she continued to peer around, Twinkle began spotting problems. Woof!

Over on the Tilt-A-Whirl, a group of birds was too small to fit under the safety bar. The pup in charge couldn't start the ride until the birds were secured, but no one could seem to figure out how to keep them safely in place.

The walkways were so crowded that the poor hedgehogs kept accidentally poking other animals with their quills. Ouch! Twinkle winced as a hedgehog bumped into a cat. The cat leaped into the air, yowling with surprise.

The lines at the food stands were long, but the Cutiecorns all seemed to be enjoying the hot dogs, cotton candy, fried dough, and other treats. Then Twinkle noticed that the goats were eating all sorts of things that weren't food! At one game booth, a goat scarfed down a mini basketball. Another ate a string of ride tickets. What a mess!

Twinkle felt that familiar lurch in her belly. It was just as she'd feared. Barking bulldogs, things were getting out of control!

Chapter 6

As she peered around the carnival, Twinkle could feel her silvery-blue horn begin to shimmer. So many things were going wrong— she needed her seeing magic to figure out how to fix them!

Twinkle felt the magic course through her, from ears to tail. Then she shook her snout. Even if her magic showed her how to fix all the different Cutiecorns' problems, she couldn't possibly solve everything all at once . . . could she?

She felt a paw on her shoulder and turned to see Glitter looking at her carefully. "Is everything okay?" Glitter asked. "Your horn is really glowing!"

Twinkle nodded, frowning. "I'm trying to use my seeing magic to work something out, but I just don't know if—"

At that moment, Twinkle spotted her mom in the distance, ambling through the crowd. She chatted with a black cat and a group of fuzzy hamsters, then waved and stepped over to a friendly pair of goats. She looked cool, calm, and completely in control—fur real! Just then, she glanced down at her clipboard and gestured for another adult pup to help her with something. The pup, a wrinkly Sharpei with an orange horn, nodded and trotted off toward the roller coaster.

"That's it!" Twinkle barked, jumping to her paws. She might not be able to fix all of the problems around the carnival by herself, but she could ask for help and delegate—just like her mom!

Glitter, Sparkle, Flash, and their two new hamster friends all turned to look at Twinkle.

"I've figured out how to juggle everything," Twinkle said quickly.

Flash's face lit up. "Juggle?" She glanced at the hamsters with a huge smile on her snout.

Twinkle held up a paw. "You're barking up the wrong tree, Flash. Not that kind of juggling!" She gestured for her friends to move in closer. "There are things going wrong all around the Furmusement Park right now! It looks like the different Cutiecorns are having trouble understanding one another, and things are starting to get out of control. I think we can fix it, but I need your help."

Sparkle, Glitter, and Flash nodded. They were all ears! (Even Flash, who seemed to have forgotten about juggling hamsters . . . for the moment.)

Once Twinkle had talked through her plan, the four pups said goodbye to their new hamster friends and left the carousel line. They walked out to the central causeway, which was lined with food trucks, game booths, and ride entrances.

"Okay, team, you know what to do," Twinkle said. She put a paw in, and Sparkle, Flash, and Glitter did the same.

"Cutiecorn crew!" they all woofed, raising their paws into the air.

Twinkle followed Flash over to the Tilt-A-Whirl, which still wasn't moving. The pup in charge looked frazzled as he tried in vain to get the little birds secured under the lap bar. "I'm afraid you just may not be able to ride on this one, friends," he said sadly.

"I think we can help!" Flash barked up, waving a paw.

Twinkle nodded. "The birds need something that will go under their wings, not just across their laps. Otherwise, they'll fly right off the ride!"

Before anyone could twitch a tail, Flash's horn began to glow. A long piece of rope coiled nearby rose into the air, wove gently under the birds' wings, and secured itself to either side of the Tilt-A-Whirl cart.

"Epic shifting magic!" the littlest red bird chirped, flapping her wings in excitement.

Flash grinned. "Thanks!" she said, giving the bird's wing a high five. "Enjoy the ride!"

Twinkle glanced over at Sparkle, who was chatting with the ticket-eating goat. As her golden horn glowed, Twinkle knew she was using her feeling magic to find something better for the goat to eat. The next minute, she was pointing a paw over at some hay bales lining the edge of the park. The goat galloped over excitedly, bleating for his friends to join him.

In the opposite direction, Twinkle could see Glitter's pink horn shimmering in the sunlight. She had a paw on the shoulder of the cat who had been poked by the hedgehog and was speaking softly to her. The hedgehog stood nearby, looking nervously down at his paws. After a moment, the cat smiled and held her paw out for the hedgehog to shake. Glitter's caring magic had done the trick!

The four pups met up back by the carousel. "Pawsome work, pups!" Twinkle congratulated them. "The carnival seems to be running much more smoothly now."

"Thanks to you," Glitter said. "We wouldn't

have known what to do if it hadn't been for your seeing magic."

Sparkle giggled. "Hey, our hamster friends finally made it onto the carousel!" Behind her, the two little hamsters bobbed by on a carousel horse. They squeaked loudly, waving their tiny paws!

"So now that everything is back under control, is it finally time for us to try some of that cotton candy?" Flash asked with a grin.

"Furbulous idea, Flash!" Glitter said. "I think we've earned—"

But Glitter didn't have a chance to finish barking before a cry for help cut through the air.

"Help! Help! It's the Ferris wheel!"

Chapter 7

Without another bark, Twinkle raced over to the nearby Ferris wheel as fast as her paws would take her. Her friends were right on her tail!

"What's—" Twinkle began. But she didn't have to finish woofing. She could see exactly what was wrong, right in front of her snout.

The Ferris wheel was spinning much faster

than it should! The animals on board were holding on tightly. Twinkle saw frightened face after frightened face move by in a blur.

Barking bulldogs, someone had to do something! But what?

Twinkle, Sparkle, Glitter, and Flash dashed up to the pup in charge of running the Ferris wheel. They could see that he was in a panic. "What happened?" Twinkle asked.

The pup, a Boston Terrier with a silver horn, turned to her with wide eyes. "I don't know!" he barked. "The wheel suddenly picked up speed—and I can't seem to slow it down or stop it!"

Glitter clapped a paw over her mouth. Sparkle covered her eyes. Flash bounced nervously. What a puptastic disaster!

Twinkle took a deep breath. "We have to do something."

"But there are Cutiecorns everywhere," Sparkle said. "Surely one of them will know what to do. We should leave this to the grown-ups."

Twinkle shook her snout. "There's no time. The walkways are crowded, and the music is loud. Most of the other Cutiecorns don't even realize that anything strange is happening!" She looked up at the Ferris wheel. "We can stop this, but we have to stay calm and work fast."

Glitter, Sparkle, and Flash straightened up and nodded. Twinkle knew she was lucky to have such pawsome friends. They were always ready to help!

"We're all going to have to work together," Twinkle instructed. "Glitter, we need your caring magic to keep the Cutiecorns on the Ferris wheel safe. Flash, can you use your shifting magic to keep the ride from moving any faster? Sparkle, your feeling magic can tell us what's making the ride spin out of control." She frowned. "And maybe my seeing magic can help us understand why."

Without another woof, the four friends stood still and concentrated hard. At once, their horns all began to glow—blue, pink, gold, and purple!

The four pups blocked out everything: the noise, the crowds, the yummy smells, the bright lights. It wasn't easy, but they each focused all of their attention on the Ferris wheel.

Glitter and Flash stood side by side, using their magic together to protect the riders and keep the wheel from speeding up. Sparkle and Twinkle scanned the Ferris wheel, letting their magic course through every piece of their fur. What could be causing this chaos?

"I've got it!" Sparkle barked suddenly. "Up there, the hamster in the blue passenger car.

Look!" She used her magic to mark the car with a swirl of golden glitter.

Twinkle squinted up at the car, looking for the hamster. Focusing hard on her magic, she could suddenly see the animals on the Ferris wheel as if in slow motion. They all looked terrified . . . except for the hamster in the glittering golden car. He had his paws in the air!

He laughed and cheered as the wheel spun around, and—

"His horn is glowing!" Twinkle said with a gasp.

Sparkled nodded. "Right. He's using his magic to make the wheel spin out of control. How do we stop him?"

Twinkle peered up at the hamster. His huge smile was almost as bright as his golden horn! Twinkle knew she needed her seeing magic to solve this puzzle. Before they could figure out how to stop the hamster, they needed to know why he was using his magic to make the wheel spin so fast in the first place . . .

"That's it!" Twinkle cried. "Remember the hamsters' boat from this morning? It was full of spinning wheels that they could run on. He thinks this is fun!"

Sparkle clapped her paws. "Hot dog, you're right! He doesn't realize that the other animals are scared, or that he's putting them in danger."

But how could they make the hamster understand—and fast?

Suddenly, Twinkle had a pawsomely crazy idea.

She turned to Glitter and Flash. "Are you two getting tired, or can you keep it up a little longer?"

"All good here!" Glitter barked.

Flash grinned. "I could do this all day!"

"Ter-ruff-ic," Twinkle said. She looked at Sparkle. "Be right back."

"Back? Where are you going?"

Twinkle could hear Sparkle's bark fading behind her as she darted forward, toward the Ferris wheel. She watched the different colored cars whip by—red, green, purple, orange. As the blue one with Sparkle's golden glitter on it approached, Twinkle bounced and wagged her tail nervously. Bow wow, this was the craziest idea she'd ever had, paws down!

It was coming closer . . . closer . . . closer . . . NOW!

Twinkle sprang off her paws and took a flying leap—right into the hamster's car!

Chapter 8

"Yikes!" the hamster squeaked in alarm as his Ferris wheel car swung back and forth.

Twinkle held out her paws to steady it, giving the hamster a friendly smile. "Sorry to startle you."

The hamster stared at her with wide eyes. He was squeakless!

Twinkle took a deep breath, trying to

focus. The Ferris wheel was still spinning fast, and she was feeling dizzy! She closed her eyes and concentrated on her seeing magic.

"I'm Twinkle," she began calmly. "I live here on Puppypaw Island."

The hamster looked at her suspiciously. "My name is Nibbles."

"Nice to meet you." Twinkle tried to ignore her lurching stomach as the Ferris wheel continued whirling around. "I wanted to talk to you because I noticed that you're using your magic to make the Ferris wheel spin faster than usual."

Nibbles grinned. "I love going around and around! Isn't it fun?"

"Oh, fur sure," Twinkle said. "And your magic is really impressive! But I think you might be scaring the other Cutiecorns on board. You're used to this, but it's new for them, and it could be dangerous!"

The smile dropped off Nibbles's face. "Dangerous?"

"I know you're just having fun," Twinkle said, tapping into her magic to help her explain things in a way Nibbles would understand. "But the other animals on the ride are really frightened. The wheel is moving too fast for them! If we don't stop it soon, they could get sick or hurt."

"Oh no, oh no!" Nibbles squeaked. "I didn't mean to scare anyone." He put a tiny paw over his eyes. "Are they all mad at me?"

Twinkle shook her head. "I'll tell you what. Use your magic to stop the wheel, and I'll help you explain what happened to all the other Cutiecorns when we get off."

Nibbles froze, terrified.

"It will be okay," Twinkle assured him. "Pup's honor!"

The little hamster nodded, then squeezed his eyes shut. Twinkle could see his golden horn sparkling even more brightly than before as the Ferris wheel slowed to a gentle stop. Barking bulldogs, what a relief!

A crowd of Cutiecorns had gathered around the base of the wheel, and they all clapped and cheered as it stopped spinning. Twinkle could see Glitter, Flash, and Sparkle in the front of the group, cheering loudest of all.

As each Ferris wheel car unloaded, dizzy Cutiecorns set paw back on solid ground.

Bunnies, birds, goats, cats, hedgehogs, and pups all looked disoriented . . . and relieved to finally be off that crazy ride! When it was Nibbles's and Twinkle's turn to climb out, Twinkle waved a paw at the other Cutiecorns who had been on the Ferris wheel.

"Could we bark with you all for just a minute?" she asked.

The other Cutiecorn riders stepped closer, looking confused and curious.

Twinkle cleared her throat. She didn't like barking in front of a crowd, but she was determined to make this right. "I know that was a bit of a wild ride," she began.

"Yeah, and that hamster is the one to blame!" a queasy-looking cat said. She pointed a paw at Nibbles, who was peeking out nervously from behind Twinkle.

"This is Nibbles," Twinkle explained calmly. She needed every bit of her seeing magic now, to help these different Cutiecorns understand one another! "Spinning on a wheel is his very favorite thing to do. He used his magic to speed up the Ferris wheel because he thought it would be fun."

"Fun? I almost threw up that basketball I ate for lunch," a goat grumbled under his breath.

"I'm so sorry!" Nibbles squeaked up suddenly. The words seemed to tumble from his tiny mouth, faster and faster. "I didn't mean to scare anyone! I was having such a furbulous time, my magic got a little out of control. I've

never met other kinds of Cutiecorns before, and I didn't realize we wouldn't like the same things."

Twinkle noticed the other animals' faces soften, listening to Nibbles explain.

"I've never met other kinds of Cutiecorns, either," a white bunny said.

A brilliant green-and-gold bird nodded. "We're all really different, but it's fascinating to learn more about all of you—even if it means getting my feathers ruffled a little!"

Twinkle smiled. Then she had an idea! She leaned over and whispered in Nibbles's ear.

Nibbles giggled. "I bet there's one thing we can agree on—ice cream! Can we all go get a treat together?"

The other Cutiecorns all started talking at once.

"That sounds purr-fectly delicious!"

"I'll bet it would taste a lot better than that basketball . . ."

"Do you think they have clover topping?"

Nibbles joined his group of new friends, laughing and squeaking. As they headed for the ice-cream truck, he turned, scampered back to Twinkle, and threw his little paws around her. Bow wow, it was the tiniest hug she'd ever gotten!

"Thanks, Twinkle," he said with a glowing grin. "Aren't you coming with us?"

Twinkle glanced over at Glitter, Flash, and Sparkle, who were watching her with proud smiles on their snouts. "I'll catch up with you," she said. "I have some friends I need to thank first."

Nibbles nodded and darted off, calling over his shoulder, "I'll get you the biggest ice-cream cone I can carry!"

Chapter 9

"Welcome, friends and special guests, to Cutiecorn Academy!" Mrs. Horne announced from the auditorium stage that evening. "We're honored to host tonight's talent show, to cap off a pawsome day of carnival fun."

Twinkle barked and clapped from the very front row.

"You'll be seeing Cutiecorns from far and

wide performing incredible feats! I've gotten a sneak peek, and I think this is really going to be something to bark about. Without further ado, let's shake a tail and get this show started!" Mrs. Horne raised her paws, and the heavy red curtain behind her was swept aside.

Flash stood in the center of the stage with a huge smile on her snout. Bow wow, she was the first act! Twinkle waved and howled at the top of her lungs.

The crowd cheered wildly as Flash went through her performance—she did lightning-fast flips and tumbles, hoop-jumping, and even some incrediwoof balancing on a rope stretched between two cones! Flash was full of energy, and Twinkle could tell she was having a totally puptastic time.

Suddenly, Flash paused and looked off to one side of the stage. Three little hedgehogs scampered out and stood in front of her, grinning. Twinkle's jaw dropped. Was Flash going to do what she *thought* Flash was going to do?

From center stage, Flash winked at Twinkle. Then, slowly, her purple horn began to glow. The three hedgehogs rose up into the air, giggling and clapping their tiny paws. Using just her shifting magic, Flash began to juggle the hedgehogs in midair! Hot dog, she was actually doing it!

Twinkle couldn't believe her eyes, but she also couldn't help the grin that stretched across her snout. The crowd cheered so loudly that Twinkle could barely hear herself think!

After another minute, Flash gently returned

the hedgehogs to the ground, and the three little bundles of spikes bowed grandly. They seemed to love the spotlight just as much as Flash! Together, the four of them raced off the stage, followed by puploads of applause.

Barking bulldogs—after that opening, Twinkle knew this was definitely going to be a talent show to remember!

One act after another took the stage, and each one got tails wagging and paws clapping in the crowd! Glitter and Sparkle were both furbulous, just like Twinkle knew they would be. But the real surprises came from the visiting Cutiecorns' performances. They did things Twinkle had never seen before!

A group of birds performed some amazing aerial stunts, swooping around the auditorium right over the heads of the audience! They even got some other animals to volunteer, and used their magic to make them soar through the air, too. Twinkle never thought she'd see the day when a goat went flying overhead!

Next, a little hedgehog in a black cape and top hat took center stage and put on a barking good magic show. He did card tricks, pulled a coin out of thin air, and even made a volunteer hedgie disappear! He was so pawsome that Twinkle couldn't tell which tricks were illusions and which ones used his actual Cutiecorn magic!

Some goats used their amazing balancing skills to create a towering pyramid by climbing one on top of the other. As they teetered there, they used magic to spin in unison. Twinkle couldn't help it—she covered her head with her paws, convinced they were going to topple down on the front row!

A blindfolded cat used her sharp senses and purrfect magic to navigate a complicated obstacle course across the stage, yellow horn glowing. She even worked her way out into the audience, deftly prancing across the backs

of seats and weaving through the crowd—all
without putting a whisker out of place! For
her finale, she used her sharp claws to climb
the curtain rope in no time flat. Then she
whisked off her blindfold and waved down at
the audience!

A large hamster choir (including Nibbles)
sang a beautiful, high-pitched song, complete

with harmony! Twinkle had come to think of the hamsters as silly tricksters, but she was swept away by their squeaktastic singing. All of these different Cutiecorns really were full of surprises!

Next, a little gray bunny took the stage. Her pink horn sparkled brightly in the stage lights. But Twinkle wasn't looking at her horn—she was looking at the whites of the bunny's eyes. The poor thing was terrified! She stood pawfectly still, frozen in place.

Twinkle gasped. No bones about it, she knew this bunny—it was Fluff, the same one she'd helped during the Welcome Parade!

Without another thought, Twinkle waved a friendly paw at Fluff. Slowly, the bunny's wide eyes moved to look at her. Twinkle gave her a big smile.

Suddenly, Fluff seemed to snap out of her fear. She recognized Twinkle . . . and smiled back! She took a deep breath, then began tapping her paws against the wooden stage in a complicated rhythm, getting faster and faster. Twinkle couldn't believe her eyes (or ears)— little Fluff was a ter-ruff-ic tap dancer!

Twinkle watched in delight, smiling so big that her snout hurt. She hadn't needed any magic to help Fluff this time. Just a friendly smile was enough to save the day!

Chapter 10

"I've never seen tap dancing like that before!" Sparkle told Fluff as they made their way down Howl Hill toward Barking Bay.

"You really were puptastic," Glitter added sweetly, giving the little gray bunny a warm smile.

It was dark out when the talent show had finally wrapped up. Now Twinkle and her friends were walking with Fluff and Nibbles back to the ferry dock. Ahead and behind, Cutiecorns of all types mingled and chatted, making their way slowly down to the water. Hundreds of stars glistened overhead, and the moon shone brightly, illuminating their path and reflecting off the bay. Hot dog, what a beautiful night!

"And, Nibbles, you didn't tell us you could sing!" Flash barked with a grin.

Nibbles wiggled his ears mischievously. "We hamsters are full of surprises."

Twinkle, Sparkle, Flash, and Glitter all laughed. "We definitely learned that today," Twinkle said.

That wasn't the only thing they'd learned! The whole day had been full of new friends and new experiences—some more fur-raising than others. But Twinkle wouldn't have traded a minute of it. She felt like she'd found something she was truly good at, and she'd helped other Cutiecorns in the process. This was the best day she could have hoped for, paws down!

As the group of friends reached the dock, they saw the different Cutiecorns' ships bobbing in the moonlight. "Well, I guess this is—" Twinkle began. But before she could finish, two little furballs launched themselves at her and hugged her tightly. Fluff and Nibbles may have been tiny, but they both gave big hugs!

"Thanks for everything today, Twinkle," Fluff said. "You made me feel so welcome here, and I couldn't have done the show without you."

"And I'm pretty sure everyone would still be mad at me for the Ferris wheel thing if it weren't for you," Nibbles added sheepishly. Then he grinned. "Instead, I'm full of ice cream and I had the best day ever!"

Twinkle felt herself blushing. "Oh, it was nothing," she said. "Meeting you two was my favorite part of the whole carnival, fur sure."

Fluff and Nibbles gave each of the other pups hugs in turn, promised to keep in touch, then waved their paws and scampered off toward their boats.

"I'm going to miss those two," Twinkle said quietly.

Glitter put an arm around her. "I have a feeling we haven't seen the last of them. Maybe we can visit their islands next!"

"Bow wow, what an adventure that would be!" Flash barked.

The four friends watched as all the different Cutiecorns said goodbye to new friends and boarded their ships. The pups on the dock waved their paws as the ships pulled away and sailed out into the night. Even as the boats disappeared in the darkness, Twinkle could still hear the calls and squeaks and squawks:

"Thanks, pups!"

"We'll see you soon!"

Twinkle squinted out at the water, watching the last shadows of the boats fade. Suddenly, she felt a heavy paw on her shoulder. She spun around to see Mrs. Horne standing behind them.

"Quite the day, wasn't it?" she asked with a smile. "I see you made some new friends."

"It was the most ter-ruff-ic day of all time!" Flash yipped. Twinkle giggled. Flash was still full of energy, even though it was way past her bedtime!

"I noticed what good hosts you pups were today," Mrs. Horne said. "You were friendly, kind, and worked hard to understand our guests—even when they did things differently. I'm proud of you all for using your magic so wisely in unusual situations!"

Twinkle glanced around at her friends, feeling warm and happy inside. They were all grinning from ear to ear!

Mrs. Horne held out a paw. Four golden charms glittered there in the moonlight. Each charm had two overlapping paw prints.

"It seems to me that you've all definitely earned new charms for your bracelets," Mrs. Horne said with a wink. "These each have two paw prints on them, symbolizing your new friendships." She attached one charm to each pup's bracelet. "Wear them well!"

"Thank you," Twinkle breathed, admiring her new charm. It clinked against the others

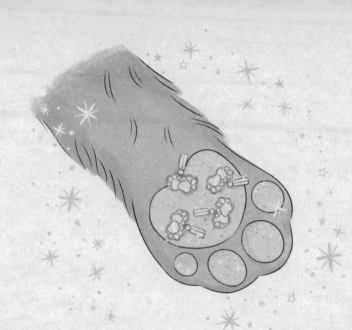

on her bracelet, making a lovely jingling sound.

"Now I think it's time for all of us to high-tail it home," Mrs. Horne woofed. "I don't know about you pups, but I think those sleepy hedgehogs had the right idea earlier. Time for bed!" With a wave, she headed off down the streets of Barking Bay.

Twinkle's paws suddenly felt heavier than giant tubs of peanut butter. She rubbed her eyes. "I think I could sleep for days."

"Oh, you don't want to do that, Twinkle," Sparkle said with a grin. She fell into step next to her friend as the four pups headed for home. "Who knows what new adventure you might miss!"

About the Author

Shannon Penney doesn't have any magical powers, but she has ter-ruff-ic fun writing about them! If she were a Cutiecorn, she'd have a turquoise horn and the ability to turn everything to ice cream. For now, she'll settle for the ice and snow of New Hampshire, where she writes, edits, and goes on adventures with her husband, two kids, and two non-magical cats.

SEE HOW THE ADVENTURE BEGAN IN
HEART OF GOLD

Chapter 1

"I'm right on your tail!" barked Sparkle, chasing her friend Twinkle across a flower-studded field.

Twinkle slowed down for a second, turned around, and stuck out her tongue with a smile. "You'll never catch me!"

Just then, another pup streaked by them in a blur of fluffy white fur. "She might not—but I will!" Glitter the Maltese puppy yipped gleefully.

Twinkle's jaw hung open in surprise. Sparkle couldn't help laughing. "Come on, Twinkle," she said, trotting up to her Beagle pal. "Get your paws in gear! Last one to the crab apple tree is an unlucky puppy!"

The two friends raced after Glitter. The beautiful horns on their heads glinted in the sunshine. After all, these weren't ordinary puppies—they were Cutiecorns!

The Cutiecorn puppies all lived together on Puppypaw Island, a special place brimming with magic and adventure. They looked just like regular puppies, but there was one big difference: They all had colorful unicorn horns! Their horns gave them each a unique magical power.

Sparkle and Twinkle ran side by side, closer and closer to catching Glitter. Sparkle put her head down, racing as fast as her powerful Golden Retriever paws would take her . . . until she heard a yelp up ahead. She looked up just in time to see a shadowy figure leap out from behind the crab apple tree!

Glitter, Sparkle, and Twinkle all skidded to a stop, so scared they could hardly bark. Sparkle covered her eyes with one paw.

"Gotcha!" cried a familiar voice.

Sparkle opened her eyes to see the grinning face of a Yorkshire Terrier with a purple horn. "Flash!" she barked. "You scared us out of our fur!" Twinkle grumbled in agreement, and Glitter giggled.

"Sorry!" Flash said, dashing in circles around

her friends. "When I saw you racing, I just couldn't help surprising you at the finish line. You should have seen the looks on your snouts!" She leaped into the air. "Plus, I have some puptastic news!"

Sparkle's ears perked up. She could never stay mad at her mischievous friend for long. "What kind of news?"

Twinkle rolled her eyes, polishing her silvery blue horn with one paw. "This had better not be like that time she said she had a special surprise, and then made us watch for an hour while she moved a bone across the table."

"That was ter-ruff-ically impressive!" Glitter protested, grinning at Flash. "It was the first time she'd moved anything using just her magic powers."